Be **Kind,**
Be **Brave,**
Be **You!**

SIMON SPOTLIGHT
An imprint of Simon & Schuster Children's Publishing Division
1230 Avenue of the Americas, New York, New York 10020
This Simon Spotlight edition July 2019
© 2018 Peanuts Worldwide LLC

Manufactured in China 0719 SCP
2 4 6 8 10 9 7 5 3 1
ISBN 978-1-5344-5473-6
This special edition was printed for Kohl's Department Stores, Inc.
(for distribution on behalf of Kohl's Cares, LLC, its wholly owned subsidiary),
by Simon & Schuster, New York.

Kohl's
Style: 54736
Factory: 123386
Production Date: 07/2019

Be **Kind,**
Be **Brave,**
Be **You!**

Based on the comic strip by Charles M. Schulz
By Elizabeth Dennis Barton
Cover art by Vicki Scott

Additional cover spot illustrations and interior illustrations by Scott Jeralds

Simon Spotlight
New York London Toronto Sydney New Delhi

Be **Kind**

If you say something kind
or do something nice . . .

. . . then you'll make someone's day
without thinking twice!

Give a gift from the heart.

And then you will see . . .

. . . being kind may take time,
but the cost is free.

When you ask for five cents,
it is kind to say "please."

(And *please* share your scarf
so your friend doesn't freeze!)

Be kind to your friends
when they want to learn.

You might even get
a **big hug** in return!

Be **Brave**

It's tough to be brave
when you're high in the sky.

It's true: You may flop,
but you also might fly!

Just take a
deep breath.

We know you
can do it!

If you think you can run . . .

. . . **you can!** Run right through it!

Be brave and **speak up!**
Defend what is good.

Use your voice. Make a sign.
And be understood.

Be **You**

Be true to yourself.
It's the one job you've got.

So dance with your heart.

Swing,

waltz,

or fox-trot!

Do you love your cool hat?

Then start a new trend!

Want to find
your own path?

Choose one with a bend.

There's only one you.

You have your own style!

So take this to heart:
The best thing to do . . .

. . . is be the kindest

and bravest,

most wonderful you!